Eva Spa____

Every new generation of children is enthralled by the famous stories in our Well Loved Tales series. Younger ones love to have the story read to them. Older children will enjoy the exciting stories in an easy-to-read text.

British Library Cataloguing in Publication Data
Southgate, Vera
    The princess and the frog.—Rev. ed.—
(Well Loved Tales)
I. Title   II. Aitchison, Martin   III. Series
823'.914[F]   PR6069.08/

    ISBN 0-7214-0766-8 (Hardback)
    ISBN 0-7214-8259-7 (Paperback)

Revised edition

Published by Ladybird Books Ltd Loughborough Leicestershire UK
Ladybird Books Inc Auburn Maine 04210 USA

The Princess and the Frog

retold for easy reading
by VERA SOUTHGATE M.A. B.Com.
illustrated by MARTIN AITCHISON

Ladybird Books

THE PRINCESS AND THE FROG

Once upon a time, there lived a king who had seven beautiful daughters. But of all his daughters, the youngest was the most beautiful.

This princess had one favourite among all her toys. It was a golden ball. She spent many hours throwing it up into the air and catching it.

Near the king's castle was a huge, dense forest. Under a big tree on the edge of the forest there was a deep, dark pool.

On a hot day it was pleasant to rest under the cool shade of the tree, by the pool. The princess often went there to play by herself.

The youngest princess used to run about on the grass near the pool, throwing up her golden ball and catching it.

One day, however, when the princess threw up her ball, it did not fall into her outstretched hands. It fell onto the grass and bounced into the deep pool with a loud splash.

The princess could not bear to think that she had really lost her beautiful, golden ball. She began to cry. And the more she thought about the loss of her favourite toy, the louder she cried.

As the princess wept, she heard a voice saying,
"Why do you weep, young princess? What is
wrong?"

The princess looked up to see who was speaking to her. She could not see anyone nearby. There was only a frog, sitting at the edge of the pool.

So she said to the frog, "I am crying because my beautiful, golden ball has fallen into this deep pool."

"Do not cry," said the frog. "I can help you to get your ball. But what will you give me if I find it for you?"

"I will give you anything you wish for," replied the princess. "You can have my clothes or my jewels or even my golden crown, if only you will find my golden ball."

"I do not want your clothes or your jewels or even your golden crown," replied the frog.

"I should like you to love me. I want you to let me be your friend and play with you. I want to sit beside you at the table, eat from your golden plate and drink from your golden cup. I want to sleep in your bed beside you."

"If you will promise me these things," went on the frog, "I shall dive down into the deep pool and find your golden ball. Do you promise?"

The princess thought that the frog was talking a lot of nonsense. Also, she wanted her golden ball very much. So she said, "Yes, I will promise all that you ask, if only you will find my golden ball for me."

At these words, the frog dived into the pool.

The frog dived deep into the pool and soon
came swimming up again with the golden ball in
his mouth. He threw the ball onto the grass.

The princess was so happy to see her favourite plaything once again. She picked it up and laughed with delight as she threw it into the air and caught it again and again.

Then she turned her back on the frog and the pool, and ran away through the forest towards her father's castle.

"Wait for me! Wait for me!" croaked the poor frog. "I can't run as fast as you can!" And he hopped along behind, trying to catch up with the princess. She did not turn round but just kept on running.

The next day the young princess was sitting at dinner with the king, his courtiers and the other princesses. As she ate from her little, golden plate, the frog found his way into the great hall of the castle. He jumped from step to step up the marble staircase.

When he got to the top he knocked on the door of the dining room. "Youngest princess, open the door for me!" he cried.

The princess ran to the door to see who was calling to her. When she saw that it was the frog, she was afraid. She slammed the door shut quickly and went back to her place at the dining table.

The king saw that his daughter was afraid. "My child, what has frightened you?" he asked. "Is there a giant outside the door who wishes to carry you away?"

"Oh no, dear father," replied the princess. "There is no giant outside the door, only a horrible, slimy frog."

"What does the frog want with you?" asked the king.

Then the princess told her father what had happened in the forest the day before. "I promised him that he could live with me," she said, "but I never thought he would come so far from the water."

Just then another knock was heard on the door and a voice cried out:

"Youngest princess, hear me call.
Remember you lost your golden ball,
As you played by yourself beside the pool.
I dived into the waters cool,
And your ball I found and returned to you.
Now please remember your promise true,
To take me along to live with you."

31

"When a promise is made it must be kept," said the king to his daughter. "Go and open the door."

The youngest princess went and opened the

door. As she returned to her chair, the frog hopped behind her. When she sat down, the frog said, "Put me on the table beside you, please."

The princess hesitated but the king told her to do as the frog asked.

When the frog was on the table, he said to the princess, "Please push your little, golden plate nearer to me. Then we can eat together from the same plate."

The princess did so, but very unwillingly. She barely touched her food and each mouthful seemed to choke her. The frog, however, enjoyed every bite he ate.

When he had finished eating, the frog turned
to the princess and said, "Now I am tired. Please
take me to your room and we will lie on
your little, silken bed and go to sleep."

At that the youngest princess
burst into tears. She did not like
to touch the cold little frog, and
she could not bear to think of
him beside her in her own bed.

Then the king grew angry and spoke sternly to his daughter. "If someone helps you when you are in trouble," he said, "you cannot afterwards turn your back on him. Take the frog with you to your room."

So the princess had to pick up the frog and
take him to her room.

She put him in a corner of the room, as far as possible from the bed. Then she got into her silken bed and turned her back on him.

Once more the frog spoke up. "I too am tired," he said. "I want to sleep beside you on your silken sheets. Please lift me up."

Again the princess began to weep. "If you do not lift me into your bed," went on the frog, "I shall have to tell the king, your father."

The princess knew she had no choice, for her father would insist that she kept her promise. So, with tears running down her face, she picked up the frog, climbed back into bed and put him on the silken pillow beside her.

No sooner had she done so than the frog turned into a handsome prince! Not only was he
handsome but he had a kind face, and he smiled
gently at the startled princess.

Then he told her how he had been bewitched
by a wicked witch and turned into a frog. The
spell could only be broken if a beautiful princess
would take this frog as her companion, live with
him, eat with him and sleep with him.

The prince told the princess how he had often watched her playing with her golden ball in the forest and how he had fallen in love with her.

"Dear princess, will you now marry me?" he asked.

The princess looked into his kind face and agreed to do as he asked.

Then, hand-in-hand, they went to tell the king what had happened.

The next day they set off in a carriage driven by six white horses. They travelled to the kingdom of the prince's father. When they arrived, there was great rejoicing at the return of the prince who had not been seen for many years.

Some time later, the prince and the princess were married and they lived happily ever after.

The golden ball was kept in their palace, inside a special glass case, and resting on a purple cushion.